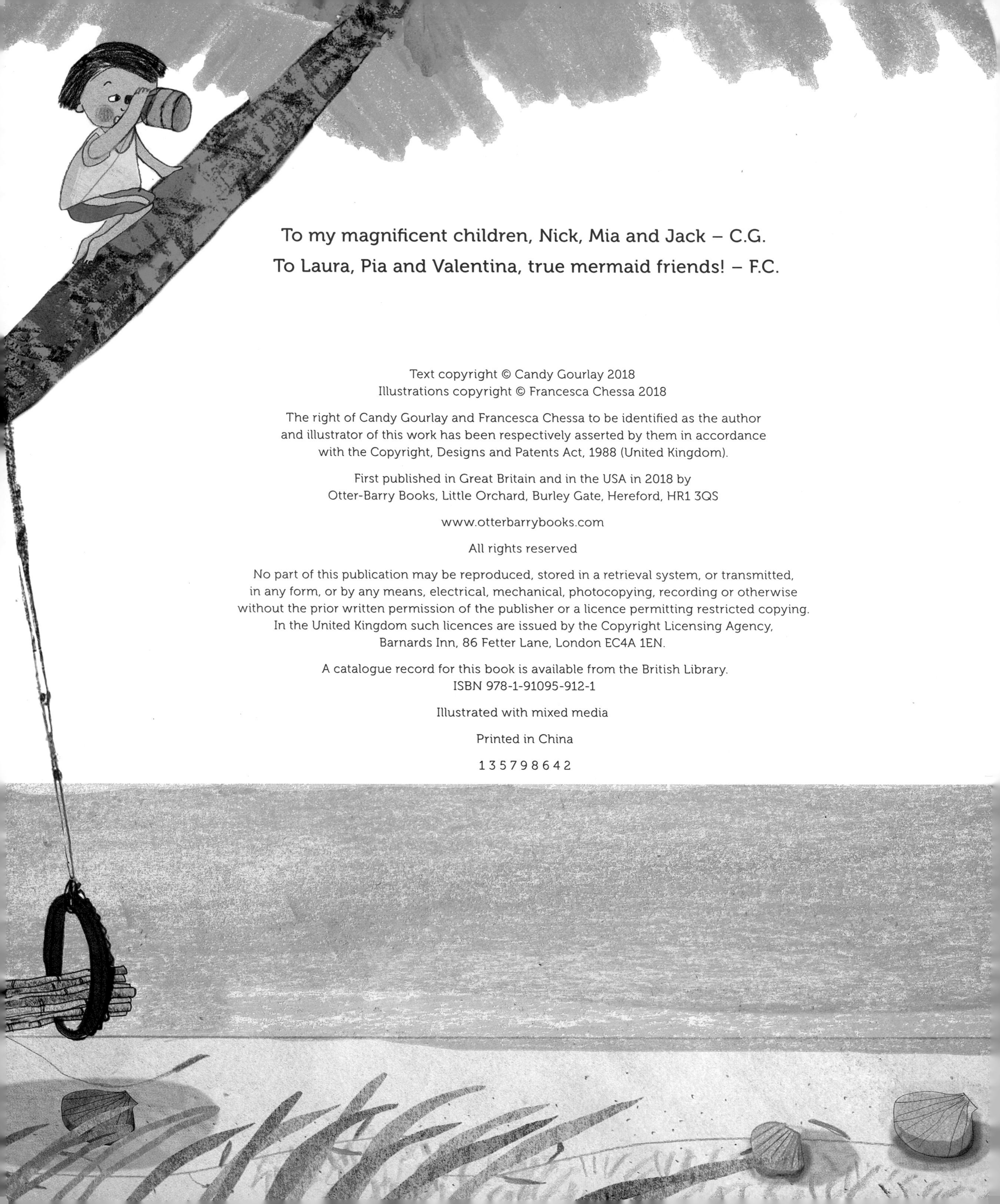

To my magnificent children, Nick, Mia and Jack – C.G.

To Laura, Pia and Valentina, true mermaid friends! – F.C.



First published in Great Britain and in the USA in 2018 by
Otter-Barry Books, Little Orchard, Burley Gate, Hereford, HR1 3QS

www.otterbarrybooks.com



A catalogue record for this book is available from the British Library.
ISBN 978-1-91095-912-1

Illustrated with mixed media

Printed in China

1 3 5 7 9 8 6 4 2

# Is it a Mermaid?

Story by

Candy Gourlay

Pictures by

Francesca Chessa

**One** morning, Benji and Bel spotted something on the beach.

"What is it?" Bel wondered.

"It?" the something replied. "I'm not an it. I'm a SHE!"

"I know what you are," Benji said. "You're a Dugong."

"Of course not, you silly little boy in a vest," the Dugong said. "Can't you see?

I am a beautiful mermaid!

See THIS? This is a mermaid's tail!"

"No," Benji said. "That's a DUGONG's tail!"

The Dugong looked hurt. Then she brightened up.

"Listen to this. . .

“STOP! STOP!” Benji cried.
“What are you doing?”

“Why, I’m singing of course,” the Dugong said.
“Mermaids love to sing!”

“Me too!” Bel said.

"You can sing all you want," Benji said.
"But it's not going to change anything.

**YOU ARE A DUGONG."**

But the Dugong was not listening.

She was **bouncing** down the beach
and Bel was **bouncing** after her.

"**WATCH!**" the Dugong cried.

"STOP!" Benji yelled. "Stop! Stop! Stop!"

"I was just trying to show you how mermaids ADORE swimming gracefully in the sea," the Dugong said.

Bel ran into the water. “I wish I was a mermaid too,” she said.

Benji ran in after her. “She’s **NOT** a mermaid. She’s a Dugong!

Look at those flippers! Those are **Dugong flippers!**

Look at that snout! That's a **Dugong snout!**

Look at that body!
That's a Dugong body!

And do you know
what a Dugong is?
It's a SEA COW."

"Oh no," Bel said. "Oh, Benji."

The Dugong tried to hide her tears
but her flippers were too short.

Benji felt terrible.

“I’m sorry,” the Dugong said.
“But we mermaids are a bit sensitive.”

“Me too!” Bel whispered.

Benji hung his head.

“It’s me who should be sorry,” he said.
“I hurt your feelings.”

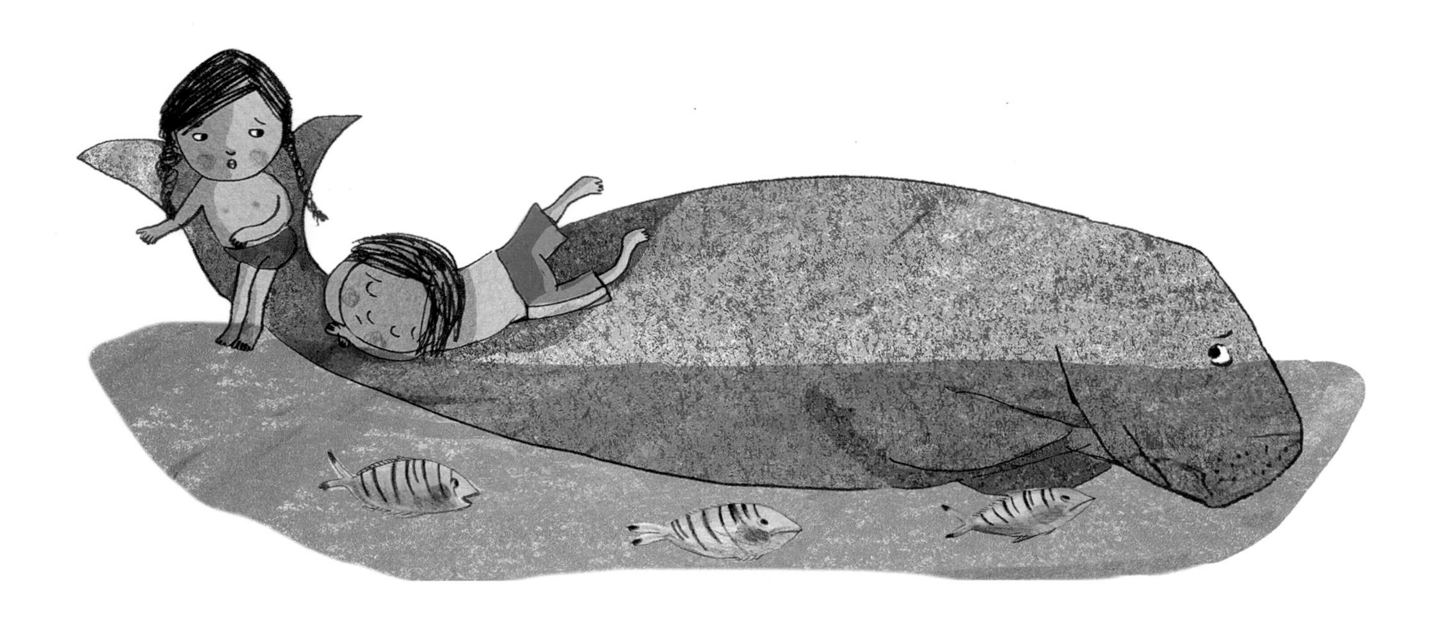

The Dugong smiled.

"It's OK," she said. "We mermaids are very forgiving."

"Do mermaids like to play?" Benji asked.

"Mermaids LOVE to play!" the Dugong said.

For the rest of the day, Benji and Bel played with the Dugong.

They sang. And swam.
And had a lovely, lovely time.

At sunset, the Dugong said goodbye.

"I have to go," she said. "Mermaids **never** stay out after dark!"

"Goodbye!" called Benji and Bel. "Will you come again?"

"Of course I will," the Dugong said.

Benji and Bel walked home as the sun sank into the far side of the world.

"I love mermaids!" said Bel.

"Me too," said Benji.

## About Dugongs

It is said that during the 17th and 18th centuries European sailors arriving on South-east Asian shores mistook Dugongs for mermaids.

In fact the Dugong is a sea cow, but the word 'dugong' is from the Malay word for 'mermaid': duyong.

Although Dugongs are called sea cows they are more closely related to the elephant. They even have little tusks hidden in their mouths and, like the elephant, they eat a LOT – a Dugong can eat up to 40 kilos of seagrass a day!

Sadly Dugongs are under threat from sea vessels and the destruction of their seagrass habitat. They have been listed as vulnerable to extinction by the International Union for Conservation of Nature and Natural Resources (IUCN).

Today, seagrass meadows are under threat around the world. Check out www.projectseagrass.org to find out how you can help save the Dugong's disappearing habitat.